# the BROTHER bias

### Tees&jeans

# HALLIE BENNETT

# BOOKS BY THIS AUTHOR

### *Standalones*
*Batter Up: An Instalove, Curvy Girl Romance*
*Wood Lessons: An Instalove, Curvy Girl Romance*
### *Tees & Jeans Series*
*The Brother Bias: A Brother's Best Friend, Curvy Girl Romance*
*The Boss Bias: An Age Gap, Curvy Girl Romance*
*The Bad Boy Bias: An Opposites Attract, Curvy Girl Romance*
### *Lumberjacks of High Ridge Series*
*Kept by the Beast: A Curvy Girl, Mountain Man Romance*
*Claimed by the Woodsman: A Surprise Pregnancy, Mountain Man Romance*
*Found by the Loner: A Curvy Girl, Mountain Man Romance*
### *Curvy College Reunion Series*
*Campus Good Girl: A Curvy Girl/Jock Romance*
*Campus Queen: A Steamy Curvy Girl Romance*
*Campus Bookworm: A Shy Girl/Loner Guy Romance*
### *Christmas & Curves Series*
*Festive Fever: A Curvy Girl Holiday Romance*

# PROLOGUE

### *ELLA*

**M**oaning downstairs breaks my concentration from reading. Andy, my older brother, invited a few friends over while he's home for the summer, but this doesn't fit the usual whooping and hollering from his buddies.

Curious, I turn the book face down on the nightstand before leaving my room to creep down the stairs and peek over the railing. The explanation for the sounds shocks me—a man and woman braced against the wall in the hallway below.

A pink sleeveless dress lies bunched around her waist, exposing a strapless bra to the man whose head is currently bent to her breasts. His own pants appear loose, threatening to drop lower while his hips piston in and out of the woman as he nails her to the wall, and the cause of the moaning becomes clear.

Familiar blonde waves of hair swish with the movement, and my stomach tightens at the realization that it's Gavin, my brother's best friend, though I don't recognize the woman. According to Andy, Gavin wasn't supposed to be home for another week, so his presence is a surprise. Another breathy gasp floats up to my position, reminding me I should leave, but I can't tear my eyes away.

Why are they doing this here? Where's Andy?

Questions swirl in my mind even as the show makes me hot and bothered—imagining myself as the mystery woman. I've had a crush on Gavin ever since Andy brought him home to play video games one afternoon years ago. Three years older and a football jock, I knew he was out of my league, but that didn't stop me from fantasizing about what it would be like to be his.

Back muscles flex with each hard thrust and grunted words burn the tips of my ears. "You like having me fuck you while our friends hang out in the basement, don't you? You're not even trying to keep quiet. Anyone could walk in on us, and that gets you off, doesn't it?"

His observation about being caught sends a skidder of guilt down my spine, but the arousal wetting my core is stronger, forcing me to stay until the girl's muffled screams get more frequent, and I can tell that they're about to finish. Comprehending my time's up, I sneak back up to my room—the thought of Gavin catching me spying unbearable.

I've hidden my crush well by avoiding being around whenever he came over. I'd hide in my room, afraid of becoming a stuttering, sweaty mess if I tried talking to him. Now, his visits are less frequent since he and Andy are juniors in college while I'm still a high school senior, but my feelings remain as strong as ever—refusing to abate just because of distance.

And now this. Endorphins flood my system at what I witnessed, and I know Gavin Cross won't be leaving my mind or heart anytime soon.

Door shutting with a soft click, I turn the lock on the knob and reach a hand down my pants to feel just how aroused my voyeurism has made me. My eyes close as I picture the scene below with a slight modification: Gavin driving his hard cock inside *me*, filling *me* up, and it makes me rub my clit harder.

His words about being found out replay in my mind, and the rush of fear at someone seeing us together spikes my desire. Who knew such a thing would amplify my need instead of dulling it?

Too soon an orgasm crashes over me, but I don't make a sound—afraid somehow he'll know what I've done. Weak legs shake as I slide to the carpet, and my eyes catch on the wrinkled Mathletes tee hanging over my hamper of dirty laundry.

Ragged breaths of pleasure seep away to be replaced by a sick knot that sits in my stomach.

*Mathletes.*

*What the hell am I doing?*

Tears well up behind my glasses before falling down my cheeks; Gavin will never want me like that. We live in two different worlds with me on Planet Nerd while he's Mr. Popular. These fantasies I make up will only ever live in my head, and the pathetic nature of that truth cuts me deep.

Climbing to my feet, I unlock the door, observe the empty hallway, and scurry into the bathroom to clean up. My reflection in the mirror stares back sad and red-faced with mousy brown hair and eyes before I glance away, disgusted.

Gavin Cross will never be mine, and the sooner I accept that fact the better.

# CHAPTER ONE

*ELLA*

TEN YEARS LATER

Sunlight beats down on my back as I wait for Saoirse and Abigail to arrive at the cafe after picking up our mobile orders. I thought sitting under one of the umbrellaed tables outside would be nice, but I'm starting to regret the decision as heat causes sweat to gather under my breasts and armpits. Air-conditioning would be preferable to this, even if it does come without a view of the park across the street.

"Hey, thanks for picking these up; I'm starving." Saoirse plops into the metal chair across from me as Abigail follows behind in her quiet manner. The three of us met freshman year of college and gravitated towards each other to the point we gave ourselves a silly moniker: The Tees and Jeans Club. Curvy introverts more likely to spend the night studying than out partying, we took comfort in our casual attire—promising to never change who we were or try to be something we weren't for attention.

Unwrapping my sandwich, I listen as Saoirse fills us in on the latest drama happening at work; she started managing the campus cafe at our alma mater after graduation. We all decided to stay in the small town—home to Smith College, although it wasn't that difficult of a choice for me since it doubles as my hometown.

"It's amazing what goes on behind the scenes there, and we had no idea as students." Abigail pipes up after taking a drink of her green tea.

"Puts a new spin on my view of some of our professors; that's for sure."

"And what about your pen pal? I want to hear about him," I say, eager to live vicariously through Saoirse since my life was devoid of attractive men pursuing me. Last Valentine's Day, the three of us had signed up for the town's matchmaking event, with little success except for Saoirse, who still exchanged letters with her mystery man.

"What's to talk about? We write letters about our lives—nothing I haven't already shared with you guys." She shrugs, but her gaze avoids ours as she focuses on scraping the last of her salad from its plastic container. Glancing up, she pins me with a probing stare and changes the subject. "I heard Gavin's coming home."

"Yeah, Andy told me yesterday. Guess he's going to take over the bar and grill once his parents retire." I haven't seen Gavin in years, not since his last visit home for Christmas. But that doesn't stop the butterflies from rousing out of hibernation.

My lone boyfriend was a fellow accountant at the private firm I work for on Main Street, and we hadn't lasted long. Poor Kyle—the reality of him couldn't compare to my fantasies of Gavin, so I'd broken it off after a couple of months of dating three years ago. Thankfully, things weren't so awkward after he'd moved on to our receptionist, Brooke.

"And the prodigal son returns...or rather the prodigal crush." Abigail jokes.

"Is that even a thing?"

Abigail nods, mock seriousness playing about her eyes. "It is when you've harbored an unwavering love for this guy with no hope of it waning anytime soon."

My foot taps against the concrete as I play with the edge of a napkin. "Love's a bit strong, don't you think? He's really only a placeholder until the right guy comes along, then I'll have a flesh and blood man and can let go." The lie rolls off my tongue easily. Maybe if I say it enough times I'll start to believe it.

But Saoirse calls me on it. "You had one of those; remember Kyle? You still couldn't shake hot as fuck Gavin Cross, and I can't say I blame you." They've only met him in passing since I still made a point not to hang around too long in his presence the few times he returned to town. But those times were enough for them to understand my dilemma.

"I said the *right guy*. Clearly, Kyle wasn't it—doesn't mean someone besides Gavin isn't around the corner."

They share a look of doubt, and Abigail slumps in her seat. "Because there's a plethora of unattached men around here."

"And if there were, we'd still struggle to speak to them."

This time we all exchange commiserating frowns. A decade later and our nerves remained a large part of our singlehood. The only reason Kyle and I had made it so far was because he asked me out point blank, and I'd thought it would be a good idea to seize the one opportunity I had—even if he didn't exactly fit what I was looking for.

"That's the upside to letters," Saoirse admits. "Writing along with the anonymity removes most of the barriers my fear erects when I'm chatting in-person with a guy."

"If only we'd all been so lucky..." Abigail sighs wistfully, watching a family at the park begin feeding the ducks. It's late summer, so most of the babies are grown, but it's cute seeing all of their feathers flap in excitement for a snack.

An alarm goes off, and I snatch my phone off the table to turn it off before gathering my trash. "That's my cue. I'll see you guys later, okay?"

They wave farewell, starting to pack their own leftovers. Tossing the crumpled wrappers of my lunch away, I leave the cafe to walk down the sidewalk to Tippen and Associates, focusing on my afternoon tasks when the sign for Anthony's Bar and Grill across the street diverts my attention. Soon, Gavin will take over the family restaurant and up my odds of seeing him everyday, with the building only a few doors down from my company's.

*Maybe it's fate.*

My ridiculous mind tries spinning a romantic tale of how we were meant to come together this way years later and grown—perhaps changed enough to garner more attention, at least on my part. He's always drawn my eye, and no amount of time or distance has altered that fact. But I'm no longer just Andy's little sister.

I'm a woman. A woman who's carved out my own path of friends and employment with hobbies and interests that fill my time.

*You're forgetting to add that you're still chubby with glasses, and those hobbies are reading fantasy romances or watching Lord of the Rings.*

A sense of melancholy pervades my body as I hasten my pace, wishing I could outrun the disheartening truth because, no, I haven't changed enough. I'm still the math nerd from high school. Hell, I turned it into a career as an accountant!

*Forget about it. Forget about him.*

No use dredging up insecurities now, and a snort of laughter eases some of my sadness as I reach the glass front of Tippen and Associates—best to save wallowing in self-pity for home not work. So, I shove all the unwanted feelings into a box and smile brightly at Brooke upon entering the office, determination lifting my chin.

# CHAPTER TWO

*GAVIN*

The drive through Smithfield soothes my soul as old memories appear at every corner. It's been over a decade since I've called this town my home, but I'm back permanently now. And it feels good.

Consulting for companies has provided a whirlwind life of travel and experience—something I'd yearned for after growing up in a small town. A flimsy plan of going pro in the NFL had kicked around my head after Ohio University offered me a football scholarship, but it didn't take me long to realize there were guys way more dedicated and talented than I was.

So when my dad mentioned turning the family business over to me again, instead of shooting him down like always, I took stock of what he said—for the first time, appreciating the opportunity—and enrolled in business management classes. Of course, dreams of exploring the world ran rampant through me once I'd graduated, but I've finally reached the point where that hectic lifestyle isn't for me anymore.

I need something more. Stability. Roots.

Pulling into the drive of a two-story colonial home, I lean against the headrest before going inside—eight hours of driving done. My parents wanted me to stay with them until I could officially move into my new apartment on the first, but thankfully my best friend, Andy, offered his childhood home as an alternative while his parents were on a cruise. Aunts, uncles, and cousins crowded my parents' home in preparation for their retirement party next week; I loved them all but didn't want to be surrounded by people twenty-four seven.

Humidity hits me in the face when I open the door, my shirt immediately clinging to sticky skin. *Damn, I need a shower.* First, the long drive and now this—something to wipe the grime away sounds perfect. Grabbing my duffel bag, I skip over the front porch stairs and knock on the door, waiting for Andy to answer. But it's not him I see.

Instead, the door opens to reveal his little sister, Ella. *Not so little anymore.* Tight biker shorts hug her hips and a crop top reveals most of her stomach and the bottom of a sports bra. The unexpected sight leaves me speechless, and inappropriate heat builds in my belly.

It's been awhile since I've seen Ella, but it's always been in a group setting with Andy present. To be honest, I'm not even sure she likes me because she disappears pretty quickly whenever I'm around. But she can't avoid me now as we stand facing each other in the doorway.

"Gavin. What are you doing here?" Her glasses magnify wide brown eyes, and I wonder where Andy is.

"I'm supposed to be staying here for a few weeks until my apartment's ready. Didn't Andy tell you?" Her blank expression tells me he didn't, but she steps back, allowing me in. The chill of the air-conditioning is a welcome relief as the unchanged foyer of the Johnson home surrounds us.

"No, he didn't." A frustrated sigh purses her lips, and my gaze drops to the pretty sight. *What the fuck?* The trip must be making me loopy because this is Andy's little sister—not a woman to get involved with. "Surprise, surprise. My absent-minded brother forgot to notify me that I wouldn't be the only one staying here. Can't imagine how it slipped his mind."

I chuckle because that sounds like Andy; his mind's always racing to the next thing, forgetting about little details such as notifying his sister of my arrival. "If it's a problem, I'll get a hotel room or something."

"No, it's fine. There's a spare room you can use upstairs, but you can bet Andy's going to hear from me." We walk up the stairs, and I try to keep my eyes from watching her swaying ass. *Goddamn, what is my problem?*

"You and me both," I mutter, though I won't be able to voice my true issue with Andy's lapse in communication. Louder, I ask, "So, why are you staying here? I thought you had your own place."

"I do, but it's flooded after the pipe behind the washer burst. It's taking them a while to fix."

"Looks like we're stuck together, then." A brief smile appears before Ella motions to the room behind her. Small but efficient, a full-sized bed and dresser occupy the space while a couple of framed seascapes decorate the walls. I haven't spent a lot of time up here because Andy's old room was located in the basement, but it's nice.

"Looks like it." She shrugs, making the hem of her tee rise higher to show a glimpse of the rounded curve of a breast before it disappears again. "I'll let you get settled; let me know if you need anything." Then she's gone before I can thank her, and my theory that she dislikes me seems to hold true.

*Probably for the best. Means I can't act on any bad ideas.*

# CHAPTER THREE

### *ELLA*

*Oh my God.*

I am going to kill Andy. I can't believe he didn't tell me that Gavin was coming to stay here at the same time as me. What am I going to do?

I manage to hold it together enough to get to my room and close it behind me before completely losing my shit, but this is only the first day. Pacing across the beige carpet, the mirror hanging over my door reflects my image and today's clothing choices—eliciting an embarrassed groan.

Shorts outlining every hill and valley of my hips and thighs with a crop top that shows my stomach and the purple stretch marks. "How's Gavin supposed to resist this?" I scoff.

If I had known he was coming... I stop that thought because if I knew he'd show up today I would have made sure not to be here. And would have resorted to sneaking around in my own home to guarantee I saw him on my own terms—perfectly dressed and mentally prepared. Instead, he catches me half-clothed in an outfit I'd never wear outside the four walls of this house, because I'm not that brave.

Granted, I've worn the biker shorts out when they're covered by an oversized tee, but I've never risked everyone seeing so much of my exposed belly in the crop top. Hell, no one's seen any part of me much exposed except for the one night I spent with Kyle—which was still in the dark and mostly under the covers.

*And not very satisfying...*

Shoving away the disappointing memory, I grab my phone and call Andy.

"Hey, sis!"

Skipping the pleasantries, I scold. "When were you planning on telling me about Gavin?"

"What about Gav? Oh, shit. He's there already?"

"Yeah, with no warning from you." Closing the blinds on my window to shut out the blinding light from the setting sun, I ask. "What's he doing here anyway? He mentioned waiting for an apartment to be ready, but why can't he stay with his parents?"

"Their house is full of family because of the party next week. Don't worry, El; you'll hardly notice he's there."

*Fat chance.*

The man is like a drug, an addiction I can't shake—the doses from our minimal interactions leaving me with a contact high that's lasted for years. Now, he's going to be underfoot for the foreseeable future; I'm not sure my poor body can take that kind of hit.

Annoyance fading to a low buzz, I sigh and take a seat at my desk. "Whatever. It's fine. Next time, try to remember to inform your sister of something that's going to affect me, okay?"

The slam of a car door sounds in the background before Andy's voice comes over the line. "You got it; sorry about the mix up. I'll give Gavin a call after this to check on him. Are we good?"

"Yeah, I'll talk to you later." We hang up, and I toy with what to do for the rest of the evening. Logically, I know it's pathetic to hide out in my room like an insecure schoolgirl, and an hour later, my growling stomach proves how unrealistic it is.

Whipping my tee off, I swap it for a longer shirt to cover my butt before hovering by the door, straining to hear any movement outside. Silence signals safety, so I cautiously open the door and enter the hallway.

Muscles relaxing, I head towards the stairs when the bathroom door opens and a wave of steam wafts over me before I slam into a hard, slick body.

"Whoa, are you okay?" Gavin grips my waist for balance and reaches another hand to fix my skewed glasses. Pressed to his chest—the drops of water glistening on his skin seeping through my cotton tee—my nipples pebble, and I resist the urge to rub against him.

"Yeah, guess I need to pay better attention to where I'm going." I joke nervously, an awkward giggle bubbling over.

"Well, it's your home, so I think this one's on me." He shifts backward to put some separation between us. The full view of his broad shoulders tapering to a defined six-pack rockets my temperature to high heat. Kyle sure as hell never evoked such a reaction from me, and he'd done a lot more than just standing in front of me naked except for a towel.

Waving a dismissive hand and moving further back, I say, "No matter; I'm glad you're settling in. I'm heading downstairs to grab something to eat. If you're interested, maybe we could share a pizza?"

*What are you thinking?*

The invitation blurts from my mouth before I consider the ramifications: spending time alone with Gavin—the exact opposite of my goal.

*What's the big deal? You want the man; maybe it's time to see if he could want you to.*

The mature part of my brain decides to make an appearance, and it's got a point. All this fantasizing stands on the shaky foundation of quick interactions and observations I've made over the years by watching him with Andy and at school. Basing my feelings on something more like having conversations with the man might be a better route to go.

*But it's terrifying.*

*Suck it up, buttercup.*

Fear and logic war inside while I try to maintain a calm facade.

"That sounds good; I'll eat whatever. But I should probably get dressed first." He grins, highlighting his handsome features, and a scarlet flush sweeps over my skin.

"Probably a good idea." I return the smile, proud of myself for stringing together an intelligible sentence. "I'll see you downstairs."

# CHAPTER FOUR

*GAVIN*

Ella scrambles away, leaving behind the sweet scent of lavender, and I return to my room—replaying the scene in my head. I'm surprised by her dinner offer, though not as much as I am by my body's reaction to having her curves plastered against me. All that softness molded to me caused the blood to rush south which doesn't bode well for the rest of this stay.

Something's clearly gone haywire with my nerves or hormones or whatever because Andy's sister is off-limits. He's never explicitly said so—most likely since she isn't my usual type—but I've assumed it's been implied all these years. And it's never been a problem until now.

It's *not* a problem. *It's a fluke.*

The doorbell rings thirty minutes later when I jog down the stairs. Ella accepts the pizza with a smaller box on top before closing the door, and the smell of pepperoni and cheese tickles my nose.

"Perfect timing." She jokes, and we walk back to the kitchen, where she sets everything down on the marble island, then grabs some plates from the cupboard. Popping the top off the smaller box, a stack of breadsticks is revealed, and my starving stomach can't wait to dig in.

"Thanks for doing this; do you want me to Venmo you?" I ask as she grabs two water bottles from the fridge.

"No, you're good. You're technically a guest; I'm sure my mom would freak if she knew I'd accepted payment for food." The Johnsons were laid back parents who always provided trays of snacks whenever I hung out with Andy, so her conclusion isn't far off. Ella sits on the barstool next to me, and we settle into a companionable silence while eating.

"So, how are you doing? I haven't seen you since what? Christmas three years ago? What's new?" I ask after finishing my fourth slice and realizing I don't know much about Ella besides the fact that she's Andy's sister. He mentioned she's an accountant, and I know she's helped my dad at the restaurant, but other than that, I'm clueless.

"Nothing much. Just working at Tippen & Associates by day and meeting up with Saoirse and Abigail afterwards. My life's not that exciting." She shrugs and tucks a stray strand of brown hair behind her ear.

"I don't believe that. What about a boyfriend?" Curiosity pushes the question out, but I don't examine why the answer matters to me so much. Her disconcerted gaze skitters across mine before dropping to her water bottle where she picks at the label.

"Nope...I used to date a guy I work with, but that ended a while ago. What about you?"

"Nothing too serious. It was hard to meet someone and build a relationship when I traveled all the time. But that'll change now that I'm back in Smithfield." Helping my parents transition into retirement and refamiliarizing myself with the business had been my top priorities before finding a woman, but the need pushes to the forefront, especially with Ella's warmth by my side while we enjoy a quiet night together.

It's a domestic scene that somehow feels right.

*No, you're not thinking clearly because of the long drive earlier. This can't be right. Think of Andy.*

"Oh, really? I'm sure your mom will be happy to hear the news along with every eligible woman within the county limits."

"Does that include you?" Flirting comes naturally, no matter how taboo. My body attunes to her every move as I await her answer.

Her head tilts contemplatively, sending chestnut waves tumbling over one shoulder, and a delicate vulnerability clouds her eyes. "Do you want it to?"

We've entered dangerous territory—alarm bells ring in my head. The slamming of the front door is followed by a hollered, "Hello", as Andy interrupts the moment and barges into the kitchen. His palm slapped my back in greeting. "Hey, man! Glad to see you made it okay. Did you guys save me any food?"

Ella hops down from her perch and pushes the half-eaten pizza towards her brother. "Have at it. I'm going to let you guys catch up; talk to you later."

"See you tomorrow," I call, but she's already long gone—reminiscent of her escape earlier after the shower incident—and the fact that she keeps running from me doesn't sit well.

"So, are you ready for Smithfield life again? I held doubts you'd ever come back for real, even with the restaurant hanging in the balance." Andy leans his elbows on the marble island top before stuffing half a slice of pizza in his mouth.

"Yeah, it'll be a nice change of pace. I've got a lot of ideas for Anthony's Bar and Grill, so it seems less like the ball and chain I imagined when I was younger and more an opportunity to build something new that's my own." While my parents never forced the family business on me—preferring I choose for myself—there'd still been hope that I'd eventually come around, and I guess they were right to keep the faith.

"Good to hear, man. I'm just glad I got my old workout buddy back. Ian's great, but he doesn't push me as hard as you do."

I laugh because our friend, Ian, is a beanpole who's better suited to writing code than lifting weights—imagining him trying to spot a two-hundred pound weighted bar for Andy is comical. "Is that all I'm good for?"

"That and serving as my wingman. I've missed the trouble we used to get up to; it's too tame around here without you." Talk of women reminds me of the particular one upstairs who's drawing me in like a fish on the line. *Speaking of trouble...*

"Well, don't get too excited. I'm not planning on picking up the torch of our rowdy high school days. Most of my days will be occupied by work."

"No problem. Nights are where it's at anyway."

Smirking, I ignore the optimistic rejoinder and start clearing the empty boxes while we continue to catch up. We don't text or call a lot, so it's nice to finally talk like old times—one more benefit of this move.

*Among other things...*

# CHAPTER FIVE

*ELLA*

A silly grin spreads on my face as I leave Gavin and Andy alone and return to my room.

*What just happened?*

I think Gavin was flirting with me, and I didn't completely melt in a puddle of nerves and embarrassment. Instead, I responded in kind, asking if he wanted me to want him?

*What the actual fuck?*

When I'm safely ensconced in my room, my fingers fly across my phone texting Saorise and Abigail about this new development. It would appear action over avoidance actually worked, and the confidence boost rushing through me made me forget past doubts to start imagining a real future where Gavin and I could be together.

"You did what?"

"You go, girl! Get your man!"

A flurry of texts light up the screen at my announcement, and the two different reactions don't surprise me. Saoirse's the more outspoken one of our group, though it's not hard to be in a trio of introverts, while Abigail is the most cautious and quietest.

We stay up late exchanging messages—something I'll regret in the morning—but this is the first real breakthrough for me. Dating Kyle had been a risk, and I'd learned a lot of things about myself through that experience. But it doesn't compare to the possibility of Gavin. The leap I took with Kyle looks like dipping a toe in the kiddie pool at the waterpark. With Gavin? It feels like a fall from the high dive into deep waters.

I just hope I don't drown.

THE NEXT MORNING DAWNS too early, my bleary eyes refusing to open as the alarm keeps beeping. I'd prefer staying warm and cozy in bed continuing a dream about Gavin, but since that can't happen, I comfort myself with the good news that it's Friday.

"Alexa, stop the alarm." Immediately, the annoying reminder stops, and I quickly get ready for the day. If there's one thing I dislike about my profession, it's the dress code. We're expected to wear business casual which means no comfy jeans which had been an adjustment from my usual attire. Now, my closet consists of skirts and blazers with button downs and polos—not the sexiest or most comfortable of looks.

Shimmying a black pencil skirt over my wide hips, I tuck a navy silk tank into the waistband before finishing the look with a striped blazer. My hair gets tied back into a serviceable bun, and I'm ready to go.

The clanging of a pan comes from the kitchen as I hurry downstairs to grab breakfast. Delicious smells of bacon tinge the air, and when I see Gavin at the stove flipping a pancake, I stifle a moan at all the goodness bombarding me. Plates of food rest on the counter, prepared to receive more as he transfers another pancake to a towering stack. The cotton of his tee strains against his shoulders while grey sweatpants mold to his butt and thighs.

*Something about a man in sweatpants...Hot damn!*

"Good morning," I say cheerfully, attempting to act normal and not like a horny teen. "Looks like you've been busy. What time did you wake up?"

Gavin shoots me a smile and gestures to a barstool before handing me a full plate of bacon, eggs, and pancakes. "Five-thirty, but I tend to get up early for a run and shower. All of this is an apology for showing up unexpectedly yesterday and to prove I can be a good houseguest." He winks at the last part, and I almost choke on a piece of bacon.

A man has no right looking this good in the morning.

"There was never any doubt," I tease after downing a gulp of orange juice. "So, what's on the agenda today besides becoming a master chef in my kitchen?"

"I'm meeting my dad at Anthony's this afternoon to figure out what needs to be done before he officially hands over the reins next week. My mom will probably be there, too, considering how I skipped stopping by the house yesterday when I got into town. What about you?" He stands across from me, consuming quick bites of food, and it feels natural sitting here discussing our plans for the day.

*Don't get ahead of yourself.*

"Well, your dad wanted me to visit and go over some of the restaurant's finances, which I thought was strange considering he usually drops by the office when he has questions. But now it makes sense: he wants me to review the books with *you*."

And showcase my nerdy math skills.

*Correction: my sexy way with numbers.*

I hide a smirk at my stupid positive spin, though there may be merit to the thought. Gavin's not dumb; he probably appreciates a woman with intelligence.

"Sounds good. Do you know what time you're coming by? I can have lunch waiting for you."

"Oh, you don't have to do that..."

"It's not a problem." His fork waves through the air as he disregards my refusal. "It's the least I can do; is there anything in particular you'd like?"

Staring at him in adoration—restrained so as not to freak him out, though I'm sure hearts float over my head all the same—I flutter my hands in a nonchalant manner. "Nope, surprise me."

*Like you've done the entire time you've been here.*

"Alright...let me give you my number and just call when you're on your way." He rattles off a string of digits, and I'm in awe that after a decade of knowing each other, we've finally progressed to being in each other's contact lists.

Is this a case of slow and steady wins the race?

# CHAPTER SIX

*GAVIN*

This week's been hell—sweet, torturous hell.

In all the years I've known Andy, and by association Ella, I've avoided any sort of awkward feelings muddying the waters. She was his kid sister, I stuck to our crowd of friends, and all was well. Except now my body's completely foregone that history in favor of lusting after her every chance it gets.

Including, but not limited to: when we share breakfast every morning, and she wears those form-fitting skirts and silk tops that outline her curves—hyping a naughty secretary fantasy that recurs in my dreams. Or when we hang out in the evenings after work, and she's changed into comfortable tees and jeans that beg me to strip her naked and start exploring.

It's pure insanity, and I'm not sure how much longer I'll be able to resist giving into these desires. The tough part is I believe she'd let me touch her if I tried. Those times Ella disappeared in my presence are gone, making me think I misinterpreted her distance all this time.

But it goes beyond the physical, too. She explained the company finances patiently, answering my questions with ease and intelligence. Her humor is smart and sarcastic—our banter fun, almost feeling like foreplay.

"Okay, I've got the popcorn." Ella walks into the den with the large bowl in preparation for tonight, and my hardening cock takes note of her swaying breasts beneath her tee. Fuck, I don't think she's wearing a bra. "Are we ready to start the next episode?"

"Yeah, sure." I stumble over the words, forcing them past my dry mouth. We've been binging a show all week, but it's the last thing on my mind at the moment. My attention hones in on Ella as she flips the light switch—plunging the room into darkness save for the light of the television—and settles next to me on the couch, the bowl of popcorn between us.

We stay like that until the on-screen couple ends up alone in a closet, and it's obvious they're about to give in to the sexual tension that's been building throughout the season. Stealing a glance at Ella, I notice the heavy rise and fall of her chest as her breathing quickens, and when my gaze lifts, her dark eyes are watching me instead of the TV.

"It's about damn time they got together, huh?" I reference the show, hoping to lighten the mood, but instead, an intimate note enters my voice as the question parallels our situation.

"Makes the payoff better," she murmurs, her body shifting towards me. Her thighs rub together, and I lick my lips, imagining her pussy clenching in need.

Moving the popcorn to the coffee table beside us, I brace an arm along the back of the couch and tentatively draw the back of my hand down Ella's cheek to her throat. A brief hitch in her breath stutters out as her head tilts slightly back, exposing the delicate line of her neck.

"Gavin?" The whisper of my name with the pleading lilt at the end is my undoing.

Leaning forward, heat mingles between our parted lips before I lower my mouth to press firmly to hers—a hand anchoring her to me with a strong grip. Heady desire swirls in my gut. Ella invites me deeper with a playful retreat, and I willingly chase, propelling her further into the plush couch cushions.

The drone of the TV in the background fades behind her soft whimpers, spurring my need to hear more. I raise up enough to slip a hand between us and over the curve of her breast, a hard nipple poking my palm through the fabric—no barrier of a bra to be found.

*I fucking knew it.*

Tweaking the tip, Ella arches into the slight touch with a gasp, her fingers fiercely clutching my arms. "That's it, baby girl. You like this, don't you?" I lick over the fragile lobe of her ear.

"Yes... God, yes... If you only knew?" A chiming jingle plays as my phone vibrates in my pocket, interrupting the moment. I try to ignore it, but the inopportune noise continues.

"Damn, I'm sorry." Frustration and desire cause my teeth to grind as I reach a hand to turn it off. The name of who's calling flashes like a beacon. "It's my mom."

"Oh, you should answer; it might be important." Ella urges me off as she raises to a sitting position—her jerky actions revealing how flustered she is. "We can call it a night and see each other tomorrow."

"Ella..."

Pausing, she brushes a placating hand over my cheek. "It's alright. Goodnight, Gavin."

I watch her leave with a disappointed sigh and swipe to answer. "Hey, Mom." Her bright voice launches into a discussion about the party, but my mind's miles away. Well, maybe not that far, I think, as my attention moves upward to where Ella gets ready for bed—wishing I were with her.

# CHAPTER SEVEN

*ELLA*

My body is on fire.

An insistent pulsing beats between my thighs—starved for Gavin's touch—and my loose clothing scratches the sensitive tips of my breasts. I can't believe what just happened.

I've kissed Gavin Cross.

Gavin Cross kissed me.

I want to repeat the words over and over again, never tiring from the undeniable truth. Closing the bathroom door, I steady myself against the cream counter and grin at my reflection—swollen lips and red marks along my neck, showcasing Gavin's handiwork.

"Good job, Ella Johnson. You were brave, and you're making your dream a reality." The pep talk may be silly, but positive affirmations are a thing, right?

I speed through my nightly routine of brushing my teeth and moisturizing before dashing back to my room. Shadows fall over the bed, and I contemplate relieving the tension in my body to make it easier to sleep. Multiple walls stand between my room and Gavin's; there's no way he can hear what I'm doing in here. Right?

Trusting that logic, I change into an oversized sleep shirt and crawl into bed, laying flat on my back and closing my eyes. An image of the den appears as I go back to being with Gavin on the couch. His hand cups my breast, and I mirror the action with my own hand—flicking the budding nipple, a ripple of pleasure makes a beeline straight to my core.

Another hand slides downward to separate my folds until slick cream helps me easily glide from my clitoris to the clasping opening below. Eager fingers circle my clit, imagining it's Gavin's rough hand instead of my own. I push the fantasy further than we got downstairs—my breath becoming harsher—when the door bursts open and Gavin's large form blocks the light from the hallway as he watches me.

A slight scream erupts as I scramble to sit up against the headboard, whipping my hand out from under the covers. "What... What are you doing here?"

"I heard you. I heard those breathy fucking moans, and I knew what you were doing. What I don't know is what you were thinking of." He walks to stand at the end of my bed and begins unbuttoning his jeans. "Want to tell me, baby girl?"

I shudder at the provocative request while my eyes stay glued to the action at his waist as he releases his erection, stroking it with a strong hand. My brain struggles to comprehend the scene before me and a garbled "What?" spills out.

"You heard me. What were you thinking? Toss the blanket aside and keep playing with yourself, too, because I want to watch as you tell me."

Like moving in slow-motion, my hand shoves the comforter off my legs and to the floor, leaving me exposed to cool air and

Gavin's hot stare. Bending shaky knees, I spread my thighs and hear his sharp inhale.

My heart pounds in my chest as I swallow hard and obey him, dipping my hand lower again. "I thought of you and me in the den," I hesitantly begin. "Your hand reached beneath my shirt like this."

"And what do I feel? Describe the weight, the softness of your breast in my palm." Moonlight plays over his dark form as he continues squeezing his hard cock.

My lashes flutter close as I focus on illustrating what he wants, but Gavin barks, "Eyes on me, baby girl." And they train on him in immediate compliance.

"It's smooth as you trace the curve, following the path of a delicate blue vein until your fingertip charts the raised bumps of the areola, skirting around my plump nipple." I've never in my life spoken this way before, but there's something to be said for a mutual masturbation session where I narrate—the explicit nature of the words affecting both of us.

"Because I prefer to tease you, don't I?" His husky whisper curls around me, and I increase the pressure on my clit, rubbing furiously—needing to come.

Licking dry lips, I jerk my head in a brief nod and attempt to think of what to say next. My brain is barely functioning during this fever dream of an evening; being expected to voice my inner seductress at this point seems like cruel and unusual punishment.

*That you're enjoying...*

"Your hand cups my pussy before driving two fingers inside without warning..."

"And your body clamps down hard, refusing to let go as I tunnel deep, adding another finger because you need something thick. Thick to stretch that tight pussy." My lips part in a short cry of relief as his guttural words send me over the edge. But I don't have long to enjoy the sensation when his weight lands on the end of the bed while his head dives between my thighs, burying his tongue into my spasming sheathe.

"Gavin!" I try to wiggle away in shock, but he holds me firmly to his mouth.

"Don't stop playing with your clit, baby girl. I want to taste another sweet orgasm from you."

*Holy fuck.*

Kyle never went down on me, so this is a new and very welcome experience as Gavin's tongue sweeps along my contracting walls. I lighten my touch, unsure how well this is going to work with his head brushing against my fingers, and you know, his tongue making it difficult to focus on what I'm doing.

But this is hotter than anything I've imagined, so I'm going to try my damnedest to keep up. Trembling fingers trace along my sensitive bud, letting it rest before kneading the nerve endings again. Another climax builds then peaks, and Gavin demands I continue—sloppy, wet sounds radiating from where he keeps his mouth planted, drinking me down until sensitivity overwhelms me.

"Stop. No more. I can't." I weakly nudge his shoulder, too tired to do much more, but he listens and lifts his head before seizing my aching hand and sucking it clean.

"You've done so well, sweetheart." He clambers over my body to nuzzle my neck. "Such a good, obedient girl. You relax for a bit, and I'll take care of the rest."

My fuzzy mind isn't sure what he means, but I don't really care as drowsy satisfaction seeps into my bones. He can do whatever he wants because I'm his.

I always have been.

# CHAPTER EIGHT

*GAVIN*

A quivering hand carefully closes Ella's legs as I help her turn to her side, adjusting myself to the curve of her back. My head is reeling in a million different directions. I've never experienced anything like what just happened, and I haven't exactly been a choir boy for the past thirty-one years. Andy hadn't been exaggerating the trouble we used to get up to.

After I got off the phone with my mom, I came up here intending to go to bed when I heard Ella through her bedroom door—obviously touching herself, and the temptation had been too much. I had to see for myself, and fuck if it hadn't been worth it.

Seeing her body splayed out for me, surrendering to my orders—it's something I'll never forget. And the taste of her... *Goddamn.* I didn't want to stop.

Now, it's my job to take care of her until she's ready to continue our loveplay. Because if she's willing, there's no chance I'm leaving without feeling her wet heat surrounding my cock.

I caress her bare leg, drawing light fingers over a shapely calf to her upper thigh before repeating the gesture and grazing a tender kiss across her shoulder. Ella's breathing is still labored, and frankly, so is mine, but I keep my touch soft and soothing.

"How are you feeling?" I whisper in her ear, desperate to know she's okay.

She yawns and cuddles closer to me. "Sleepy. Satisfied." Bending her head back, Ella's brown eyes meet mine, and I realize I haven't seen her without glasses yet—it feels more intimate seeing her without the barrier. "What about you? I kind of clunked out before you could ?"

I place a shushing finger over her lips. "Don't worry about me. If you need time to recover, I'm happy to just lay here with you." The unfamiliar sentiment flows freely; I wouldn't say I've been a selfish lover in the past, but I usually don't linger in a woman's bed. I've definitely never felt this sense of contentment from just spooning.

Ella stretches a hand back to steer my head towards hers for the most breathtakingly reverent kiss I've ever experienced, and a tremor of vulnerability shatters my heart. We part reluctantly, our lips clinging to each other in longing.

"I want you in every way, Gavin—to give you what you need." I read the truth in her imploring gaze. How can I refuse her?

Feathering a kiss over her forehead, I concede. "We'll take it as slow as you need. If it's too much, we'll stop. Okay?"

She nods, and I quickly remove the last of my clothing before rejoining her in bed. A thought for protection rears its untimely head. "Damn, I don't have a condom, but I'm clean."

"So am I, and I'm on birth control. We're good."

Sighing in relief, I elevate her leg to brace against mine, widening her enough to let me enter from behind. My hand cups her mound to find the sticky residue leftover from earlier, and I tentatively draw a finger over her clit causing her to twitch and moan.

"Easy, sweetheart." I hitch my hips along hers and poise the tip of my shaft to her center. "I plan on loving you for a long time."

*Fucking.* I should have said "fucking", but loving Ella doesn't seem so far-fetched. Not after the week we've spent living together. And not after the intimacy we've shared.

My cock inches deeper into her consuming warmth, and once fully seated, I start a languid rocking motion. The floral scent permeating her room mingles with the smell of sex creating a unique blend, and it feels like we're in our own little cocoon detached from the world.

Her hair tickles my cheek as I nibble the lobe of her ear before dipping my tongue lower to lick and suck the fragile line of her neck, hoping to leave behind something to mark her as mine.

Ella's hand grasps mine tightly, holding it to her chest, and the frantic beat of her heart matches mine. "I feel so full..." She writhes in my arms, following my brief retreat before surging forward again—maintaining the languorous pace.

"I'll take that as a compliment." I chuckle, a bit of pride billowing in my chest. Her pussy contracts, and I realize she's close. This position primes her perfectly for me to hit her g-spot on every stroke, and soon, our slow ride culminates in a ravaging orgasm for both of us. Hot spurts of cum coat her pussy.

For a second, I envision it taking root—Ella pregnant with our child.

*Don't be ridiculous. This isn't permanent.*

The errant thought evaporates as my groan of satisfaction pierces the air. I never want to leave this bed...or Ella.

THROUGHOUT THE NIGHT, I reach for the beautiful woman beside me, ignoring all the reasons we shouldn't be together. Yet, in the dim twilight of morning, regret threatens to overpower me. Bitter bile rises up, but I swallow hard.

*What have I done?*

Ella sleeps soundly next to me, and I steal another touch of her downy cheek before easing out of bed and getting dressed. Serene quiet blankets the room. If only the same could be said for my tangled emotions—a mess of loyalty to Andy and yearning for Ella.

Exhaustion weighs on me making it impossible to think straight or try to unravel the web of issues, but there's no time to rest before I need to launch into my morning routine. Maybe the familiar tasks of a workout and shower will clear my head. Help me form an explanation to give Ella when I have to tell her a relationship between us is impossible.

I can't betray Andy that way. He trusted me with his sister; I took advantage. And there's no excuse for it except pure lust and this raw desire to be near her.

# CHAPTER NINE

*ELLA*

I stretch upon waking, sore muscles reminding me of the night before. An old meme of Ron Burgundy saying, "Well, that escalated quickly" runs through my mind since Gavin and I jumped from a first kiss to sex in the span of an evening. But can it be considered fast if it's something I've wanted for over a decade?

My hand searches for Gavin but comes up empty, and I crack my eyes open to see all signs of him gone like everything had been a dream. Snatching my phone off the nightstand, I check the time to see it's almost nine, and I remember how he said he starts his days early, which would explain his absence. It would've been nice if he could've made an exception today, though, because I'd have liked waking up next to him.

*Maybe tomorrow.*

Confidence that there *will* be a tomorrow after another evening spent with Gavin startles me as it's the antithesis to my usual point of view, but there was a genuine, intimate connection between us last night. I don't believe he lied when he whispered sweet promises, and I won't chalk them up to being caught in the moment.

His sincerity was real.

Typing a bombshell message to Saoirse and Abigail, I hit send and wait for the deluge of replies to flood my phone—it doesn't take long. Their excited congratulations for finally "getting my man" make me smile. There's still Andy to contend with when he discovers his best friend and sister are together, but I doubt he'll voice too much dissent. He's all about going with the flow and letting people make their own decisions.

Not too worried, I drag myself out of bed, lamenting not being in better shape as my muscles twinge again, and prepare for a busy day. The retirement party for Gavin's parents is tonight, and I agreed to help decorate beforehand.

No one's downstairs when I descend, though I find a covered plate of waffles in the fridge with my name on it. A warm flush suffuses my skin at the kind gesture from Gavin. All week, he's made sure I've eaten, even when I'm working late or miss breakfast with him. The culinary side of him was a nice surprise. Despite his family owning a restaurant, Gavin never seemed to have any interest until now, and my work with him has been strictly confined to finances, not the kitchen.

I finish eating, then drive to Anthony's Bar & Grill, where I see Gavin's car sitting alone in the parking lot. We must be the first ones here in preparation for tonight. A rush of sudden nerves makes me jittery as I step inside the empty dining area.

"Hello? Gavin?" Roaming back towards the manager's office, the door swings open to reveal him dressed casually in jeans and a green henley. *Damn.* I can't believe this man was in my bed a few short hours ago. How'd I get so lucky?

"Hey, I wasn't expecting you." He carries a box full of streamers and other party supplies to the closest table and sets it down before pulling random items out.

"Did you forget I offered to help get things ready for tonight? Last night really did a number on you, huh?" I tease with a playful swat to his arm until he side steps away—keeping his eyes averted. My smile falters at the intentional move, and a small pit develops in my stomach. Retracting my hand, I apologize. "Sorry... Did I do something wrong?"

An awkward pause builds before Gavin's hands clutch the sides of the box tightly, white knuckles clear. "Last night was a mistake."

Color drains from my face, and the pit grows in size, resembling a bowling ball. "I don't understand. I thought you enjoyed ?" A wave of emotion forces me to stop mid-sentence as my eyes burn with burgeoning tears.

"I did, but it can't happen again. It shouldn't have happened in the first place. Andy's my best friend and your brother; I can't betray his trust this way."

"But Andy won't care," I say stupidly. *At least I'm not the problem.*

"You can't be sure of that, and I won't risk our friendship for something that may not even work out. He generously let me stay at your parents' house as a favor, and I repaid him by fucking his sister." I flinch at the harsh explanation of our actions. Somehow, it dilutes the intimate connection, reducing it to just sex—a physical release that meant nothing.

"You know Andy; he's not the type to hold grudges or judge. Especially not when it comes to the happiness of the people he loves. What about everything you said when we were together?"

"I shouldn't have said those things; they weren't fair to you. There's no excuse because I know better. I'm sorry." His apologetic blue eyes make me feel nauseous as I read the seriousness in them. He's not changing his mind; he won't fight for me. I'm not worth more to him than my brother, which shouldn't come as a surprise, yet my romantic heart yearned for a happily ever after—for love conquers all and trumps brotherly camaraderie.

Goes to show how foolish I am.

Swallowing hard, I try to bow out gracefully before my emotions get the best of me. "I understand. I'm going to wait outside until more volunteers arrive; Saoirse and Abigail should be here soon."

He dips his head in acknowledgment, and I leave at a steady pace, though my legs want to sprint away and never come back. In my car, I drive to a more secluded part of the parking lot to park and lean against the steering wheel, pain wracking my body while silent tears fall.

*Stupid. Stupid. Stupid!*

Thoughts of this morning and the embarrassing amount of joy I felt mock me. Of course, the one time I decide to trust, it explodes in my face. I really believed Gavin would be mine—years of longing coming to fruition. *How pathetic.*

Someone knocks on my window, and I recoil, turning away and wiping furiously at my cheeks.

"Ella, are you okay? Why are you parked all the way over here?" Abigail's concerned voice is better than a stranger's, though I prefer no one to ever see me crying.

Unlocking the door, I motion for her to get in on the other side. Once she's settled and sees the evidence of my sob session, her eyes widen. "What happened? What's wrong?"

"Gavin... He..." Exhaling a ragged breath, I attempt to calm down and try again. "He said yesterday was a mistake. He doesn't want to mess things up with Andy and ended things. Though, we barely got started, so there wasn't much to end, but yeah..."

"Oh, I'm so sorry." She pats my shoulder, the small space restricting any further comforting. "That's terrible of him. Andy shouldn't have the power to dictate his life or yours."

My shoulders lift in resignation. "Apparently, he does. According to Gavin, their friendship is more important than any possible relationship between us." Another gush of tears swell at the reminder.

"Then he's not the one for you," she states firmly. "You deserve better, and now, he's freed you to find someone who will appreciate you. Maybe this crush can finally be put to rest."

She makes valid points. When I'm calmer, maybe I'll let them console me, but it won't be today. We sit there for another fifteen minutes until Saoirse arrives and Abigail tells her the news. Suitably angry on my behalf, she threatens to give Gavin a piece of her mind, but we manage to restrain her.

"I don't want to cause a scene. Let's just get this over with; we'll help decorate then attend the party tonight."

"And you'll stay with one of us, if you're unwilling to kick Gavin out of your home," Saoirse asserts, her temper flaring as bright as her red hair. Agreeing, I double-check my appearance in the rearview mirror, and we shuffle back to the restaurant where a group has already started working.

Gavin's hanging a banner with the help of Andy, and I make sure to avoid him the rest of the afternoon while my friends form a protective wall around me.

*Only a few more hours, then you'll be away from him. You succeeded in limiting your interactions before this week; you can do it again after.*

# CHAPTER TEN

### *GAVIN*

"**Y**ou've done well, son; thank you for this." My dad gestures towards the large crowd of people dancing in the center of the room and mingling on the sidelines. Everyone accepted their invitation to the Cross retirement party, and it looked like it would continue deep into the night. Unfortunately, I'm not in such a jovial mood after my conversation with Ella earlier today.

The heartbreak in her eyes will haunt me for a long time to come.

She stands surrounded by her friends at a table, and my gaze can't help hungrily roving over her lush curves accentuated by the red dress she's wearing. I want to find a dark corner, flip the skirt up, and fuck her until she forgets how much I hurt her. But I can't.

Tearing my attention away, it lands on Andy twirling some girl around—a stark reminder of why.

"Son? Gavin? Are you okay?"

Refocusing, I plaster on a cheerful facade. "Of course. Why wouldn't I be? I'm glad you and mom are having fun tonight; you guys deserve it."

"Don't change the subject. Tell me what's going on. It's the Johnson girl, isn't it?"

Denial and shock vie for supremacy as my shoulders straighten. "Why would you say that?"

"I'm not blind. This afternoon I thought there was something going on with the way you two circled each other, and tonight you haven't been able to keep your eyes off her for more than a minute. So, tell me. What happened?" His perceptiveness rankles; I don't want to talk about this when the decision has been made. But I know he won't let it go.

"You really want to ruin your party by discussing your son's problems? It's supposed to be your night," I dodge, hoping to put him off—to no avail.

"Humor me. I don't mind sparing time for you, especially when it's clearly about something important. So, lay it on me." He leans back in his chair and takes a sip from his beer, patience and determination emanating from his reclined form.

"Nothing can happen between us—me and Ella."

"Because of Andy?"

"Don't sound so skeptical. He's my best friend, and she's his little sister. I've known them for years; I'm not going to upset that balance by trying anything with her. What if it doesn't work out?" I voice my fears, my temperature rising as blood pumps through my pounding heart. The worst-case scenario would be a relationship between Ella and I ending badly, and Andy being forced to choose her side.

I wouldn't only lose her; I'd lose my best friend.

"But what if it does? She could be the love of your life, and you'd miss it because you're afraid of what Andy might think?" Dad shakes his head with a clucking of his tongue. "I've known that boy for as long as you, and he's a good friend, good man. Even if he's resistant at first, eventually, he'll come around. But if he doesn't, a woman to share your life with beats hanging out with buddies. Call me old-fashioned, but that's how I feel about the situation."

"Even if I decide to try, I've already told her it's impossible. I hurt her, Dad. I'm not sure it's fair to approach her again with a change of heart." I watch as Ella laughs at something her red-headed friend said and longing pangs in my soul.

*God, I want her.*

"Son, I hate to spoil the illusion, but it hasn't always been rainbows and butterflies between your mother and me. A loving relationship has its ups and downs where you hurt each other. You learn to apologize and forgive." His wise eyes trail over me before catching on Ella. "Looks like your girl's leaving. Here's your opportunity; what are you going to do with it?"

I ping between him, Andy, and Ella before settling on her retreating form. *I'm going to get my girl.* Jumping to my feet, I thank my dad with a brief shoulder squeeze and race after Ella.

Catching up to her outside, I grab her hand and pull her to a halt. "Ella, wait."

"Gavin? What are you doing? Please leave me alone. I don't want to hear anymore about how we can't be together." She tries twisting her arm away, but I use her momentum to propel her body into mine before turning and trapping her against the brick of the building. Light from the parking lot doesn't quite reach us, so we're wreathed in shadows—perfect since I don't want an audience.

"Wait, please. I made a mistake. I was an idiot for letting you go, and I'm here to correct that colossal error in judgment." Her struggling stops and skepticism is written all over her face.

"What changed? Have you spoken with Andy? Because it doesn't make sense that hours ago this was a betrayal of trust, but now you're cool with it." Animosity seethes from her, but I know I've earned her distrust.

Tangling a hand in the hair at the back of her neck, I angle her head, so she heeds my words—read the truth in my expression. "My dad talked sense into me. I haven't mentioned anything to Andy yet because it doesn't matter. You do." Exhaling a heavy breath, I continue. "Baby girl, you are worth fighting for, no matter the opinion of your brother or anyone else. I want you. I'm fucking falling for you. But I was too blind and stupid to trust the feeling. To trust the strength of what's between us. To know it can overcome whatever obstacle comes our way, including Andy. Please tell me I haven't irreparably fucked this up."

A sheen of tears surface, and I brush a tender thumb under her eye. "God, please don't cry, sweetheart. I'm so sorry; I never want to hurt you."

Ella's hand cups mine as she swallows hard, the corner of her mouth lifting in a semblance of a smile. "It's okay. I'm okay. I just wasn't expecting... any of this." She waves a hand between us before dropping it over my heart. "You really mean all of that? You're falling for me?"

Shyness shines bright, and for the first time today, hope peeks its head out. *Maybe we'll be okay.* "I meant every word, and I'll prove it, too, if you'll let me."

"And if Andy disapproves?"

"Screw him. He's my best friend, but he'll need to get on board real fast when it comes to the woman I love." My firm tone brooks no argument, and this time, a genuine smile spreads across her pretty face. Impulsively, I crush a swift kiss to her mouth, our teeth clashing, but I don't care. It's been too long since I've tasted her.

"I've been in love with you for years," she admits when we part. And bewilderment creases my brow.

"But you always disappeared when I visited."

"Because I was afraid of embarrassing myself or that you wouldn't be interested in a nerd like me. I've been crushing hard for a long time."

I'm stunned, but I reason, "You're sexy smart—don't cut yourself short. And maybe it's a good thing you never showed interest back then. It would've been hard to stay away, and considering our age difference, a lot of what I would've done to you would be considered illegal."

She laughs and smacks my arm. "You're not that much older, and it would've saved me years of pining."

"Well, we can make up for that now." My hand sneaks under her dress and tugs at her panties. Heat radiates from her core, and I can't wait for it to envelop my hardening erection.

"Now? Like in the parking lot?" She glances around nervously but doesn't stop me from divesting her of the lacy underwear. Indeed, the undulating of her hips indicates her hearty approval for the scandalous proposition.

"You got a problem with that, baby girl? Because I don't think I can wait to get you back home." Testing her wetness, my thumb circles her clit before unzipping my jeans and pushing my boxer briefs down, wasting no time pressing the tip to her soaking pussy.

If our first time was slow and sweet, this was going to be the exact opposite—a hard fucking to claim what's mine.

I just need her consent.

Then one moaned word echoes in the air: "Yes", and I power my way home—Ella's shout cut off by my mouth covering hers in a searing kiss of possession.

# CHAPTER ELEVEN

*ELLA*

Gavin Cross is falling for me.

Gavin Cross is fucking me against the building like a Viking of old claiming his prize.

And, yeah, I'm here for it.

Commanding thrusts shove me into the rough brick at my back, the discomfort highlighting the intense pleasure centered between my thighs. I scratch at Gavin's scalp, needing him closer as our bruising kiss mimics the pounding harshness of his thrusts. This is a vast difference from before, but I'm not complaining.

I wanted him to take me, fight for me, show me I'm his, and he's passing with flying colors. Our public location fades to the background—my senses attuned to each drag of Gavin's cock through my throbbing walls, to the bite of his teeth on my lower lip.

"You're so hot, so tight—choking my dick because you want my cum, don't you? You need me to fill this pussy, baby girl? Leave you sticky and full, the proof of my ownership running down your thighs?"

*Damn, he's got a mouth on him.*

My thighs wrap around his waist, urging him deeper. "Yes, please... I want it all... I'm so close..." Words puff from my laboring chest, staccato and short, but I think he gets it because he rubs my clit faster as his hips pick up speed.

This is raw and dirty. No pretty words or sensual exploration. Just Gavin and Ella.

Another swipe of his thumb, and the dam breaks, a cry of pleasure erupting as my orgasm shoots out like a bolt of lightning. Gavin's not far behind me, his vigorous movements becoming choppy before he growls at his release. True to his word, I feel the warm jets of his seed overflow from our joining and coat the inside of my thighs.

My legs fall bonelessly to the ground, and I'd follow their lead if it weren't for Gavin's firm body holding me steady. Fluttering soft kisses along his collar bone, I revel in my ability to do so freely. These fantasies I've had of him don't need to live in my head any longer because I got the man; he's mine.

We still have hurdles to scale like my brother, and I'm sure my own niggling doubts will rear their ugly heads again. But I'm optimistic about our chances. Gavin's willing to try, and if I held onto my crush for ten years without it relenting, I can only imagine the depths of my perseverance now that I have him.

"You're something else, Ella Johnson." He murmurs with a light peck to the end of my nose.

"You're not too bad yourself, Gavin Cross." Standing there catching our breaths, a memory flashes in my mind, and I chuckle at the irony. "You know, I've caught you in this position before."

He lurches back sending a strand of hair flopping over his forehead. "What are you talking about?"

Tucking it aside, I grin. "When I was a senior in high school, you visited Andy during a break. I was reading in my room when

I heard suspicious sounds coming from downstairs. So of course, I checked it out and found you having sex with a woman in the foyer. Against a wall, kind of like this."

Chagrin etches his features. "You saw that?"

"Yep. It was very enlightening... Not to mention it fueled a lot of fantasies afterward." His cock twitches inside me, and the power I seem to wield over him makes me bold. "Actually, I crept back to my room right after that and finished what you started, so to speak."

"Fuck, Ella." His husky exclamation thrills me. "You can't say things like that while we're still standing naked in this parking lot. At least let me attempt to get us to privacy before telling me all the times you got off thinking of me."

"Oh, cocky, are we? But there's no denying you're right, though it'll be difficult for me to recall all the times. That's a lot of years and long sessions with my hand or vibrator or..."

"Enough." A rough hand covers my mouth. "We're going home. Now."

He pulls out, a sucking noise resounding between us, and steps back to zip his pants while my skirt drops to my knees. Taking my hand, he drags me across the parking lot to his vehicle. "I hope you have everything you need from inside because we're not going in to retrieve anything."

"I'm good. I'm yours for the night."

"Wrong. You're mine for life."

Gavin yanks me to him for a fierce kiss before ushering me into his car, and I smile.

*Whatever you say, love. Yours for life.*

# EPILOGUE ONE

*GAVIN*

ONE YEAR LATER

Bells ring signaling the afternoon hour, and I straighten my tie in the floor-length mirror. Today's my wedding day—a day I've waited months for while Ella insisted on doing everything properly—and anticipation runs through me at seeing my gorgeous bride.

"Are you ready? Lifetime of commitment; it's a big step." Andy comes into view behind me, adjusting his own suit. "Though you're marrying my sister, so you damn sure better be ready."

After all the fuss I made over Andy's reaction to hearing about me and Ella, it turned out to be for nothing like my fiance likes to remind me. He'd taken it in stride, surprised but happy for us. And I'm thankful I listened to my dad that fateful night or else I would have fucked up and lost the best thing to ever happen to me.

"You don't need to worry about me; I've been ready for months now. It's your sister who's been dragging her feet." Not that I truly mind. Whatever my girl wants, she gets. Period. Even if it means prolonging the moment when I can finally tie her to me permanently.

"Women..." He shakes his head in confusion. "All this fuss over one day. It's just a bunch of flowers and shit; what's the big deal. The marriage is binding whether it's done here in church or at the justice of the peace's office."

"Couldn't have said it better myself," I agree. A knock sounds on the door before my dad walks in. The murmur of conversations from our guests filters inside before he shuts the door and gives me a hug.

"Proud of you, son. You picked a good one."

"A great one," Andy pipes up, crossing his arms over his chest.

"A *great* one," Dad amends with a wink. "We're all set outside, if you're done in here."

Nodding, the three of us leave the small room on the side of the altar. I go to stand to the left of the pastor while Andy hurries to join the bridesmaid he'll be escorting. Organ music permeates the sanctuary, signaling the joyful occasion. Wooden doors swing open towards the back of the church, and the congregation turns to watch as my niece and nephew amble down the aisle, spreading flower petals and holding the rings. Paired couples follow behind at a sedate pace—Ella's best friends, Saoirse and Abigail, along with Andy and Ian.

Soon the music changes, and Ella moves to the center of the aisle. My heart stops as breathing becomes difficult. White lace forms to her body, a deep vee plunging between lush breasts, and I'm frozen as she walks towards me.

This is the woman I'm marrying. The woman I love. And I can't believe how fucking lucky I am.

For years, I didn't notice her as anything more than my best friend's little sister, and I've kicked myself numerous times for the error. Thank God her apartment needed fixing the same time

I arrived in town last year or else who knows what would have happened? Though, I have a feeling we would have ended up on this same path—no matter what.

Ella belongs to me, and I'm meant to be hers.

Once she reaches me, her dad places her hand gently in mine, and we face each other as the pastor begins citing the vows. The comforting drone becomes a faint buzzing in my ear while I mouth the words "I love you" to my bride.

A pink flush blooms from her chest to her cheeks inspiring a triumphant grin at the sight, appreciating how responsive she is to every little thing I say or do. Her hand squeezes mine in an effort to get me to behave, and I obey...for now.

But tonight will be a different story. I'll be free to love and tease my wife for as long as I want—leading to forever.

I can't wait.

# EPILOGUE TWO

*ELLA*

TWO YEARS LATER

Sweat drips down my cleavage as I eagerly hurry inside the house to escape the summer heat. I already hated summer weather— give me winter and snow any day—but this pregnancy has amplified everything. My temperature has gone haywire, either too hot or too cold, and honestly, I'm over it. Unfortunately, I still have four months to go before I give birth to our baby boy.

*Can't come soon enough.*

The quiet of the house along with the chill rush of air conditioning eases my slight discomfort. Everyone's at my parents house for the Fourth of July, but I'm reaching a point where I am people'd out, and I wish Gavin and I could just go home for the evening. Forget fireworks.

A strong arm wraps around my expanded waist, and I recognize the gentle touch of my husband. "You doing alright, baby girl?" he asks, protective instincts dialed up to one hundred ever since we found out we're having a baby.

"Yeah, just got a little overheated as usual." He lifts the hair off the back of my neck and blows a soft breeze over the sweaty skin causing a shiver to rattle down my spine.

"Want me to take your mind off of it?" The suggestive tone makes me curious, and my hormones jump to attention. They weren't kidding when they said pregnancy makes you crave sex more than usual, and I already craved Gavin a lot.

"What did you have in mind?"

He leads me to the foyer at the front of the house before slowly twisting me around until my hands brace against the wall. "If I remember correctly, a certain spy happened upon an intimate scene years ago. I'm thinking she might need some more material to work with."

"Oh?" My legs spread after he prompts them to part, and I'm grateful I decided to wear a sundress today for easy access.

"You see, it was pretty naughty of her to keep watching such a private act. Makes me think she wants some of the same." His breath whispers over my temples as rough fingertips part my folds and glide through the budding moisture.

"Hmm... You might be right," I tease, arching my hips to tempt him into action.

"Of course, things are a little different now," he warns, fingers pumping inside me at a leisurely pace. "You're in a delicate state." His other hand pinches my engorged nipple, breasts extra sensitive during this time, before dipping lower over my rounded belly. "I'm not sure you can handle such a rough ride right now."

I moan at the decree. "I promise I can; I won't break."

"No," he tsks. "I think you need something a little softer for such a tender pussy."

The warmth of his body at my back disappears, and I wonder where he's gone when the back of my dress lifts, his hot breath puffing across my exposed center.

"I think this is better, don't you, baby girl?"

Coherent sentences elude me, but I nod—my muttered "yes" reaching him in the silence.

"That's what I thought." His tongue licks through me in an unexpected surge causing me to yelp at the shock. "Remember, Ella: we're not alone here. Anyone could walk in and see me on my knees—eating my wife's ripe pussy, face buried in her cunt."

I convulse at the filthy language. And I almost wish someone would walk in and discover my man pleasuring me. Wish everyone would know how much I belong to him. But that's crazy possessive hormones talking.

His tongue burrows deep and flicks against my walls, encouraging me to squeeze tight in an attempt to hold him, but he retreats and laps at my throbbing clit. Biting the knuckle of one hand, a keening whine gets stuck in my throat. I push my ass further back, driving my core into his mouth, trying to ride his tongue to satisfaction.

Gavin doesn't refuse me, hands holding me firmly before spanking a butt cheek. "Gavin!" I gasp at the spark of pain.

He chuckles darkly. "Don't worry. I know we're working on borrowed time; I'll play with you more later," he promises and returns to where I need him most. His licks become more insistent before sucking harder on my clit in a rhythmic push and pull. Soon the tension in my body releases and I hiss at the relief—my bones liquefying and exhaustion setting in.

Gavin continues to clean me up with his mouth then rises to his feet, cuddling me closer with sturdy arms encircling my waist. "You feel better, baby girl?"

I sigh and turn for his kiss. "Mmm... much, but now I need to take a nap."

"That can be arranged," he says and starts leading me upstairs to my old room.

The place where it all began.

"Have I told you lately how much I love you?" My head leans against his shoulder as we enter my room, and he helps me get comfortable on the bed before curling behind me.

"Not in the past hour." A tired smile responds to his joke, and I kiss the arm pillowing my head.

"Poor baby. That's much too long." Nestling deeper into the safety of his muscular form, I say some of my favorite words. "I love you, Gavin. You take such good care of me, and I know you'll do the same for our child." A yawn overtakes me.

"Sleep, sweetheart. I love you, too. More than I ever thought possible."

Contentment bursts in my heart, fatigue pulling me under, as I lay safe in the arms of my husband, brother's best friend.

My forever crush.

# Don't miss Saoirse's story next in The Boss Bias!

*Saoirse Shane's got a secret.* For months, she's been writing a secret pen pal and sending him sexy boudoir shots. Flaunting lush curves in silk and lace makes her feel powerful, but she fears what her mystery man will say if he ever found out who she was...

*A curvy girl who's inexperienced with men.*

*Thomas Moore loves a challenge,* and starting a new job at the local college seems like the perfect fit. Until one of his employees looks strangely familiar...

A fiery redhead with curves for days but who's way too young for him.

*A relationship between them is against the rules, but rules are meant to be broken, right?*

*What do you get when you pair a curvy girl and her silver fox boss together? Hot insta-love with light daddy kink and spanking in this quick, steamy romance!*

# THANKS FOR READING & DON'T FORGET TO RATE/ REVIEW!

Please consider leaving a rating/review on Amazon, Goodreads, Instagram, TikTok, and/or any other sites you review on. Ratings & reviews are the #1 way to support an indie author like me.

They don't have to be long or even positive (though I hope you enjoyed this book!). All the algorithms care about are QUANTITY.

The more reviews, the more my books are shown to other potential readers!

And they serve as guides to readers on whether or not to take a chance on an indie author.

I appreciate your support!

**XO, Hallie**

# ABOUT THE AUTHOR

Hallie prefers steamy, insta-love stories where curvy girls are claimed by filthy-talking heroes. And when she ran out of reading material, she decided to write her own stories. If you want a quick, hot read, she's your girl!

www.ingramcontent.com/pod-product-compliance
Lightning Source LLC
Chambersburg PA
CBHW030357180626
46812CB00007B/2922